T. REX TROUBLE!

For Mom and Dad, and in memory of Joe Orlando
—E.D.

For Victor Paul
—D.S.

To Dad, who always encouraged me to draw
—M.D.

T. REX TROUBLE!
A BANTAM BOOK 978 0 857 51127 0

Published in Great Britain by Bantam, an imprint of Random House Children's Books
A Random House Group Company.

This edition published 2012

1 3 5 7 9 10 8 6 4 2

Copyright © 2012 DC Comics.
DC SUPER FRIENDS and all related characters and elements are trademarks of and © DC Comics.
(s12)

RHUK26799

Bantam Books are published by Random House Children's Books,
61–63 Uxbridge Road, London W5 5SA

www.**kids**at**randomhouse**.co.uk   www.**totallyrandombooks**.co.uk   www.**randomhouse**.co.uk

Addresses for companies within The Random House Group Limited can be found at:
www.randomhouse.co.uk/offices.htm

THE RANDOM HOUSE GROUP Limited Reg. No. 954009

A CIP catalogue record for this book is available from the British Library

Printed in China

DC SUPER FRIENDS™

T. REX TROUBLE!

By Dennis "Rocket" Shealy
Illustrated by Erik Doescher,
Mike DeCarlo, and David Tanguay

BANTAM BOOKS

Dinosaur fossils
are on parade in the city
of Metropolis.

Lex Luthor has a plan.
He sprays the T. Rex
with his super foam.

Foam covers the bones.

The T. Rex comes to life!

ROAR!

Lex rides the T. Rex.
He makes more dinosaurs
come to life.

The Pteranodon flies!

The Triceratops stomps!

The Flash sees the
dinosaurs.
He calls the Super Friends.

The Pteranodon grabs
the Flash.
The Flash cannot get away.

The dinosaurs
scare the people.

Lex takes their money
and valuables.

The Super Friends arrive.

Batman says,

"Stop right there!"

Lex orders the dinosaurs to attack.

The dinosaurs charge
at the Super Friends!

Batman lassos the Triceratops.

The dinosaur bucks.

Batman holds on tight!

Green Lantern saves
the Flash with a tornado.

Green Lantern sets the
Flash safely on the
ground.

Superman fights
the T. Rex.
Its mouth is
full of sharp teeth!

Superman keeps its jaws from snapping shut!

Batman sees
a delivery van.
He has an idea.

Batman steers
the Triceratops
into the van.

Meat and fish
pour out of the
delivery van.

The dinosaurs

run towards the food.

The Pteranodon and the
T. Rex start to eat the food.

The Flash grabs Lex!

Lex's plan has failed.
The Super Friends
have made friends
with the dinosaurs!

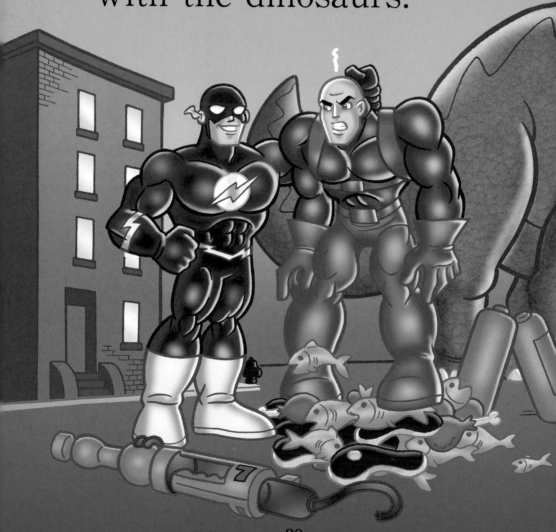

The Super Friends build
a home for the dinosaurs.
Everyone cheers!